SKIN CRAWLS

Gordon Brown

Skin Crawls

First Printing

ISBN 978-1-970860-01-6

CUTTLEFISH
BOOKS

For my mother,
who taught me to read and write despite
tears, kicking, and screaming
(on both of our parts)

SKIN CRAWLS

Nobody Lives in Haunted Houses

haunted house
her skin crawls
off to another room

spiders crawling over their eyes the garden gnome

finishing the lullaby
a voice beneath the bed

in the next room
there are cannibals
also

ghost town
the sound of someone
missing

all through the night
Mother cradles the baby
she doesn't have

blind cat
always staring
just over my shoulder

starless night
outside my window
the lady from the painting

bathroom mirror
waiting for my reflection
to smile back

Christmas Eve
the chuckles
that ooze
down the chimney

Mother's Day
she named you
in her suicide note

longest night
sound of footsteps
on an empty street

seance
the absolute stillness
of the planchette

Dreams of a Crimson Season

autumn morning
rising early
crematorium smoke

there used to be
an exit here
corn maze

autumn moon
shines soft on the car
that followed you home

champagne and roses
and zipties
crime scene photo

he cadaver dog walks toward a murder of crows

morgue basement
loopy cursive
on the toe tags

autumn evening
the moon has a new face
too

friday night
the mortuary down to a skeleton
crew

closed casket
the gravedigger's
dirty nails

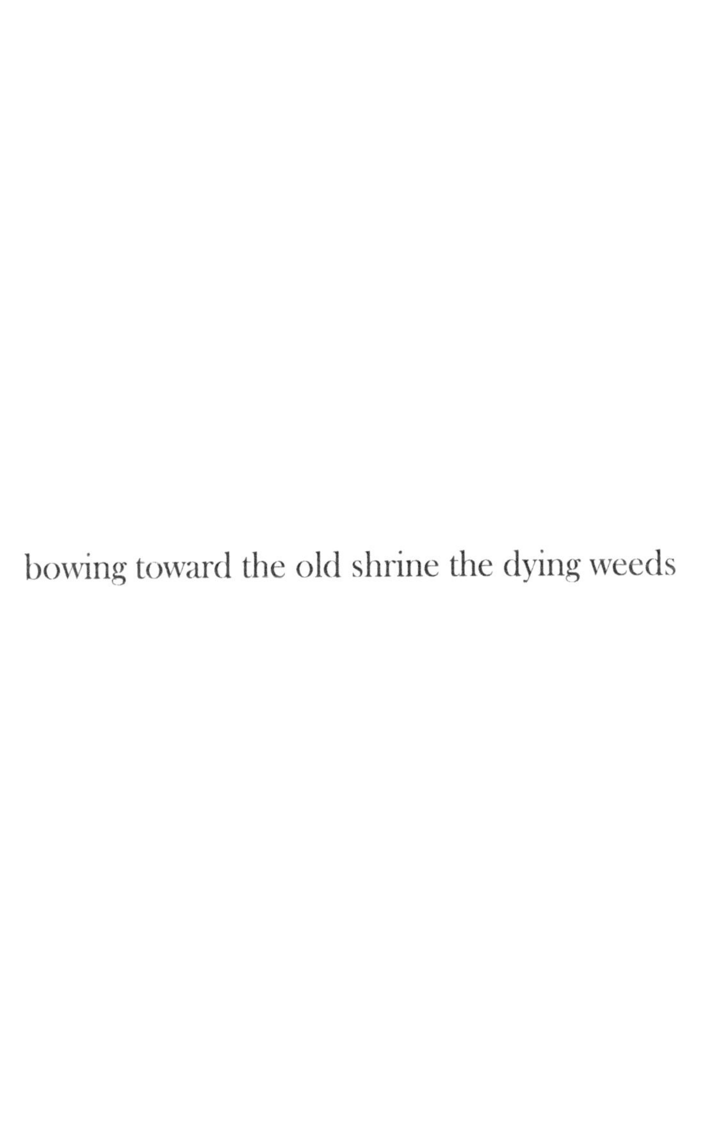

bowing toward the old shrine the dying weeds

naked and pale
in my basement
a mannequin

crimson season
all the graveyard's
crooked teeth

four days after Halloween
the little ghost
still comes to my doorstep

The People's Republic of Worms

*(these ones
lay eggs
under fingernails)*

a beetle
crawls through his chest
old scarecrow

extended family
reunited
mass grave

spring morning
the frog is motionless
and smells of formaldehyde

introduced
to the swimming hole
leeches

car accident
the embalmer does what she can
with what she has

field trip
tip of my tongue
human botfly

trail of ants
we buried the body
too shallow

mosquito song
on an unlit porch
blood relations

inevitably
there's no more song in them
cicada husks

broken skin the itch just keeps on itching

still unnamed
the twin
I ate in the womb

wet cough
bringing up
more worms

ABOUT THE AUTHOR

Gordon Brown grew up in the deserts of Syria and now lives in the deserts of Nevada. Since arriving in the New World, his work has appeared in Tales to Terrify, Weird Horror Magazine, Chthonic Matter Quarterly, Modern Haiku, and elsewhere. He spends his time writing feverishly and looking after his cats, of which he has none.

9 781970 860016